Is It an Earthquake?

Read-to-Me™

The Letter People® and Read-to-Me™ are trademarks of ABRAMS & COMPANY Publishers, Inc.

Visit our Web site at www.letterpeople.com

Printed in the United States of America   ISBN: 0-7665-1205-3

    1 2 3 4 5 6 7 8 9 0   1 0 9 8 7 6 5 4 3 2

                                                                              085401E

Is It an Earthquake?

Written by Sallianne Norelli   •   **Illustrated by Dean Yeagle**

One day, something strange happened in the Land of the Letter People.

CRASH! Mr. B jumped up. A jar of beautiful buttons fell off his shelf. The whole house was shaking!

"Oh, bother!" he cried. "Is it an earthquake?"

Meanwhile, Mr. M was about to munch.
Plop! Drop! Suddenly, the meatballs jumped
right out of his sandwich!

"Holy mackerel!" he exclaimed. "Is it me,
or is this an earthquake?"

At about that time, Ms. A was picking apples. BONK! An apple hit her on the head!

Boink! Boink! Boink! Apples tumbled down from the trees! Ms. A's ladder rocked from side to side.

"Are we having an earthquake?" she wondered.

Just then, Ms. P was feeding her pigs. Splat! The next thing she knew, she was in the pigpen!

"That's just perfect! Now I'm covered with mud!" she frowned.

The ground shook and shook. Ms. P tried to stand up.

Splash! Splatter! She fell back into the mud.

"What's happening?" she cried. "It feels like an earthquake!"

BOOM! BOOM! BOOM!

She heard a loud noise. It was coming from Ms. E's Exercise Gym!

11

At the same time, Mr. D was doing his dazzling dance. Suddenly, the floor started shaking! He slipped and fell—right in the middle of his flamenco!

"Oh, dear! Is it an earthquake?" he shouted.

Mr. D grabbed his phone and called Ms. W at the Weather Watch Station.

"What's going on?" he asked. "Are we having an earthquake?"

Ms. W caught her mug just as it was about to slide off her desk. Things were falling all around her.

"According to my instruments," she said, "the shaking is coming from Ms. E's Exercise Gym. I'm heading over there to see what's going on. I'll let you know."

"That sounds dangerous!" said Mr. D.

"I'll be careful," Ms. W promised.

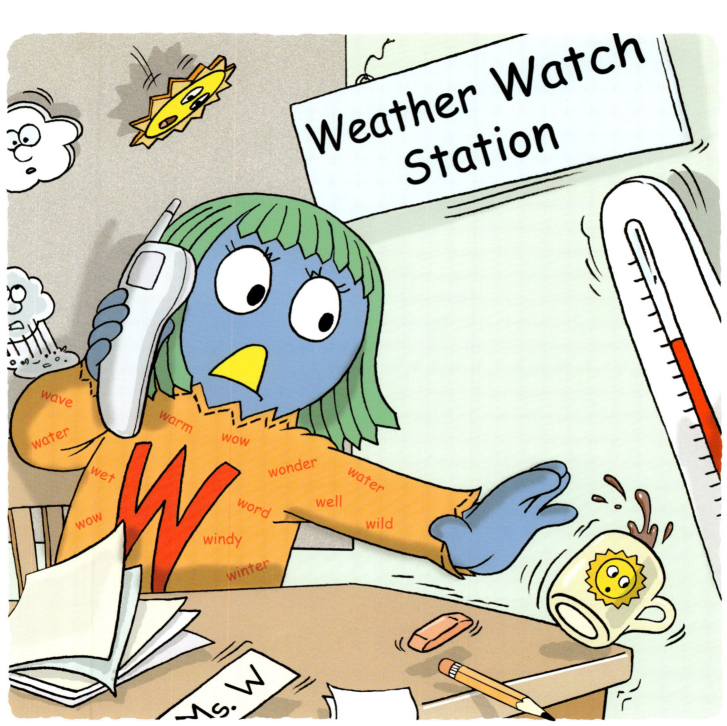

17

As quickly as she could, Ms. W made her way to Ms. E's Exercise Gym. The closer she got, the more the ground shook. By the time she reached the front door, she could barely stand up!

Ms. W carefully entered the gym. Then she started to laugh.

Gym

20

"Oh, my!" Ms. W chuckled. "I thought we were having an earthquake!"

"I'm sorry," Ms. E said. "Today is the first day of my elephant exercise class. I didn't mean to scare anyone."

"That's OK," Ms. W said, "but I think the elephants need a gentler kind of exercise."

Ms. E thought for a moment. "I know exactly how the elephants can exercise without shaking the ground," she said. And then she yelled . . .

23

"EVERYBODY IN THE POOL!"

The Letter People Company

a division of
ABRAMS & COMPANY Publishers, Inc.
61 Mattatuck Heights
Waterbury, CT 06705
www.letterpeople.com
1–800–227–9120

🎤 Read-to-Me™

Who Will Help Ms. A?
Beautiful Buttons: A Biography of Mr. B
The Clue (Mr. C)
The Dinosaur Detective (Mr. D)
Is It an Earthquake? (Ms. E)
The Fib (Ms. F)
Where Does the Garbage Go? (Mr. G)
The Right Day for a Haircut (Mr. H)
Incredible Insects: A Poetry ANThology (Mr. I)
The Jazz Jamboree (Ms. J)
KABOOM! (Ms. K)
Ha! Ha! Ha! (Ms. L)
The More the Merrier! (Mr. M)
Not Now, Mr. N!
The Opposite Obstacle Course (Mr. O)
The Perfect Pet (Ms. P)
I'm Glad I Asked (Mr. Q)
Real Friends (Mr. R)
A Super Day for Sailing (Ms. S)
Time for a Taxi (Ms. T)
There's No Space Like Home (Ms. U)
Ms. V's Vacation
Weather Watch (Ms. W)
I'm Different (Mr. X)
Just for You (Ms. Y)
Who's New at the Zoo? (Mr. Z)